Reality
of Fear

Reality of Fear

THERESA EDMUNDS WILLIAMS

authorHOUSE®

AuthorHouse™
1663 Liberty Drive
Bloomington, IN 47403
www.authorhouse.com
Phone: 1-800-839-8640

Published by AuthorHouse 11/14/2013

ISBN: 978-1-4918-3692-7 (e)
ISBN: 978-1-4918-3693-4 (sc)

Library of Congress Control Number: 2013920729

chapter 1

"Kendra, I am running late, I want you to make sure the kitchen is clean before you go to bed". Never getting a reply; Nicole rushed out the door to catch the bus to work.

Kendra calls her friend to vent. "Hey Stefani, It's me Kendra! Girl, my mom is really trippin with all the do this do that! I am so tired of all this, I feel like I'm her servant and all she does is work! Why do people have children anyway, to be their slaves"?

Stefani really didn't take Kendra seriously; this is a normal phone call vent day. "Well don't do nothing stupid girl, you got it made." What Stefani didn't know is that Kendra was very serious; she also didn't know that Kendra had talked to a friend about leaving home and was packing what she could take in a few bags.

"Hey girl I got to go, "Kendra said as she packed her favorite shoes and grabbed up some of her moms jewelry to sell for cash. This was not normal for Kendra to steal, but her friend told her that she will need to have cash for food and Kendra felt that she deserved it for all the hard work her mom demanded of her.

As she packed up the last of what she was taking with her; she called her friend Minnie, "All's a go, I'm ready now". "Alright girl, be there in twenty minutes," Minnie squealed before hanging up the phone.

Minnie pulled up fifteen minutes later, hopped out of the car and knocked on the door. "Why didn't you just blow the horn"? Kendra asked as she hauled bags out the house. "Kendra, do you really want all your neighbors peeping out the windows, putting a make on me and the car to tell your mom what you left in and what I look like? You know how your booshie neighbors are in this booshie neighborhood", Minnie laughed while helping Kendra load up the car. "Besides, are you sure you're ready for this kind of life?"

"This kind of life"! "Is there something she was not telling me?" She made it sound like it was going to be smooth sailing and I'm gonna have it made .... no rules, no parents, being my own boss. Who would pass up an opportunity like this? So off they drove, to great adventure and good times, 'or so she thought'.

They rode for over an hour before Kendra asked where they were going. Minnie laughed, "Girl! You worry too much. No worries right? I'm taking you to see someone to get rid of that jewelry, you're gonna need pocket change to hold you for a while and you will need to get a bus ticket."

Tired and hungry, they stopped in the next city, cashed in the jewelry and grabbed a quick bite to eat. They made it just in time to get a bus ticket; next bus leaves for Florida in thirty minutes. Kendra had no idea that she would be getting on a bus headed out of state, she thought she would still be close enough to home ...... just in case. Minnie saw the worried look on Kendra's face, "Trust me girl, do you really think I would let anything happen to you? My cousin is cool; she lives in Florida and has her own place. I told her your situation and she would love for you to be her guest. I have to get a few things straightened out here but will be there in two days, I promise".

With that being said, Kendra and Minnie talk about all the adventures waiting for them in Florida. Being a small town girl from Alabama; anything was an adventure.

REALITY OF FEAR

The bus finally pulled up. Kendra loaded her bags into the luggage area; Minnie gave her a tight hug and told her she'll see her in two days. Kendra got on the bus and off she went to the easy life of no mom, no rules, being her own boss.

chapter 2

Minnie needed to get her friends car back to him so off she went in the opposite direction. Since she will be headed to Florida in a few days to meet up with Kendra; she will need to get her hands on some fast cash. Kendra knew Minnie always had money her pocket, when asked; Minnie would say "my cousin that lives in Florida sends me money all the time". This was so far from the truth. Minnie pulled up in her friend's driveway, "Hey Josh!" I've got your baby back safe and sound!" Like all guys; Josh checked the car for dings and dents that he did not personally put on the 2002 Chevy Impala.

"Sooo Minnie? Did you get your friend off safe and sound?" Minnie frowned at Josh, he knew how Minnie earned her money and what kind of plans she had in store. "And what kind of lie did you tell her to get her on that bus to Florida to go live with someone you barely know?" Kendra frowned again "Mind your own business! Kendra will be fine! Besides, I will be there in two days!" Minnie told Josh how she made Kendra believe that she was going to be staying with her cousin in Florida and how they were going to have good times with no rules. Josh laughed hard and loud before asking "and who is this cousin the two of you will be staying with?" Jackie, Minnie stated .... And all went quiet.

Josh stopped laughing; he looked at Minnie for a minute before saying. "You sent her to stay with Jackie? Are you nuts"!

Jackie was nowhere close to being in Minnie's bloodline, cousin was far from the truth. She was not the type of person a mother would send any child to live with, not even for a couple of hours. Josh didn't want anything to do with Kendra being sent to Florida nor did he want anyone to know that it was his car that got her to the bus station.

Kendra lived a sheltered life in a very nice upscale neighborhood all her life. Josh was very worried about her and hoped that she would be okay. He was not trying to appear soft or look worried but the truth is; he was very worried. "You need to bring her back. I didn't know you were going to send her to Florida with Jackie. Minnie! Do you hear me? This is not good! Get to her as soon as you can!"

Minnie well understood what Josh was saying and knew she needed to get to Kendra as soon as possible. She headed to the spot where she'd been living for the last year and a half; she didn't have anywhere to really live ...... She was a runaway too!

When she arrived to the spot she called home, she was greeted at the door by a tall dark man. Shouting at the top of his lungs and very mad he asked Minnie where have she been and if the package is on its way. "Yes, she got on the bus over forty-five minutes ago and I really wish you didn't refer to my friend as a package". In two seconds Minnie felt a sharp blow to the right side of her face before her small frame was slammed into the wall. Sir was choking her with one hand, "don't ever talk back to me, you hear me! Next time you even think about what you are going to say when I ask you something I want you to think. Will this cost me my life?"

He released Minnie's throat and she fell to the floor gasping for air. "Yes Sir, Yes Sir" was all she knew would be safe to say. She didn't say another word until Sir asked her what time she will be leaving for Florida. "I told her I'll be there in two days". Sir shook his head, "two days? You know how Jackie is; you need to get there as fast as you can. I have a few errands for you tonight and I need you on the first bus out of here tomorrow morning. Make sure you check on her! Let her know when you will be heading her way. Now go fix my dinner while I get these plans together for tonight.

Minnie fried some pork chops, cooked rice and gravy, corn and fresh baked biscuits. Sweet tea was a must with every meal served. She knew exactly how Sir liked his meals, staying under his roof for six years. Minnie endured beatings at night and being locked in the closet for hours at a time as punishment when Sir's demands were not followed as ordered. Staying with Jackie was no vacation either. Jackie came to Sir as a runaway, once she turned eight-teen he sent her to Florida to expand his business.

After dinner; Minnie washed the dishes and bolted upstairs as Sir demanded earlier that evening. "The kitchen is clean Sir". "Minnie, I have two envelopes. I want you to take these envelopes to the addresses written on this paper. Envelope number one need to be delivered first; a lady will answer just give it to her. You will be handed another envelope to bring back to me, leave it in the car before you deliver envelope number two. Envelope number two is very important, be sure to give it to the person who answers the door, there will only be one person there so there is no confusion. Hand him the envelope, don't say anything. Now take the keys to the car and go straight there.

Minnie took the envelope, grabbed the keys and left the house. It took her twenty five minutes to reach her first destination; she got out of the car and knocked on the door. The Minnie handed her the envelope and waited as she walked away. The lady came back to the door with sealed envelope, handed it to her, turned and closed the door. She reached her second destination in fifteen minutes. A tall fair skinned man answered the door; he was foreign and spoke with an accent. "May I help you?" he asked. She didn't say anything, she did just as she was told and handed him the envelope. The foreign man read it, nodded his head and opened the door for her to come in, "Have a seat." She sat patiently waiting, a minute later he returned with another envelope (sealed) and placed it on the coffee table. "Minnie is it?" "Are you thirsty?" Yes I am, Minnie said with a soft voice. The foreigner went to the kitchen and came back with two bottles of pop. He spoke to her in a kind voice "Aren't you too young to be out this time out night?" It was only nine PM but she answered politely "I had to deliver this for Sir; he said it is very important".

The foreigner moved around the room and sat next to her, "Take this back to Sir and tell him thank you". He grabbed her, pulled her close to him, Minnie tried to push him away but he asked her if she read the letter. "It was open, did you not read it?" Minnie did not read the letter before giving it to the foreigner; he gave it to her to read. "I understand, she said".

There are no words for what was going on in Minnie's mind at that moment. She kept telling herself that one day she'll have enough money to set out on her own and never look back. "If it's the last thing I do, I'll make sure Sir gets what he deserves"!

chapter 3

Kendra's mom stepped off the bus after working sixteen hours. Carrying her bag; she walked a half a block to her house. She was so tired that she did not notice the porch light was off and the house was completely dark until she stepped in and closed the door. She turned on the lights and looked around, "Look at this filthy house! My daughter is going to be on serious punishment!" She stepped in the kitchen, dishes everywhere. Extremely disgusted; she dragged herself upstairs to peep in on her daughter. Nicole was too tired to get into a long drawn out argument with her daughter of not doing what she was told, what bothered her most is she has never seen the house look this messy. "Maybe this is her way of rebelling; I will deal with her in the morning". Still thinking of all the mess; she forgot to peep in on Kendra but instead went straight to her room to shower and hit the bed. "I'll deal with her in the morning!"

Seven o'clock AM............... The alarm clock is blaring off in Kendra's room. Nicole lifts her head. "After coming home to a dirty house last night, do she really want to push my buttons? Kendra!!!!!! Turn that alarm off!!!!" No response. Nicole drags herself out of bed, goes to her daughter's room, shove the door open to discover she was not in her room. Wondering if she was already up and downstairs grabbing a bite to eat before school; Nicole proceeded to the kitchen ..... Kendra wasn't there either. She went to her daughter's room and noticed that her books were still in her room, clothes were missing from the closet and the dresser draws. Nicole couldn't think straight, she couldn't think at all. She went to her room and threw on some clothes, when she turned to the dresser to grab her keys she noticed that her jewelry box was open and several valuable pieces were missing. She called several of her daughter's friends parents; no one had seen Kendra since yesterday. Nicole dialed 911.

The police arrived and ask her lots of questions, the last time she saw her daughter was before she went to work the day before. "I work long shifts and sometimes overtime, this is not supposed to happen. Do you think someone took her?" The police told her that they will need to search to house for clues and talk to the neighbors just in case they saw something.

Kendra and Minnie left so fast, none of the neighbors saw either coming or going. Nicole filed a missing person's report and several friends helped her post picture of Kendra all over town.

Nicole called a friend to pick her up; they searched all over where Kendra would normally hang out. After school was out; she went to talk to Kendra's best friend Stefani. Nicole is sobbing so badly, Stefani could barely understand what she was saying. "Stefani? Kendra is missing, have you seen or heard from her? Please!!!! If you know anything, help us find her!" Stefani thought of the conversation yesterday, "She did call me to vent about always having to do everything but I didn't really pay her any attention because she always calls me to vent about something. We didn't talk long, she said she had to go and got off the phone." Nicole turned toward the door then looked back at Stefani with tears streaming down her face, "Please call me the moment you hear from her".

Back at home, Nicole straightened the house and cleaned the kitchen. She felt like she was losing her mind so she did everything she could think of to keep busy. The phone rang; she hit her toe on the coffee table trying to get to the phone, it was the police department. "We have an eye witness that stated he may have seen your daughter in the car with another young lady. He does not know who the driver was nor did he see the license but he did say the car was blue and that the car was headed out of town.

Nicole could not think who this person may be or why her daughter would be headed out of town. "What is going on? Why didn't she call me? Who is this girl she was riding with?" too many questions, no answers. She called her job, took a week off and set out to get answers. "Somebody saw my daughter leave this house; and I am going to find out whom"!

chapter 4

Minnie didn't sleep well last night; all she could think about was her encounter with the foreigner and waking up to a five AM alarm clock going off didn't make it any better. Sir told her to set her alarm clock to five o'clock AM to make sure she caught the earliest bus out of town, and she was ready to leave. She got up, showered and grabbed her bags; Sir was waiting downstairs. She called Kendra, "Kendra! Hey, it's Minnie. I am on the way!" Kendra squealed with delight.

The ride to the bus station was very long; neither of them spoke a word, all she could think about was getting away from Sir, even if it was just for a little while.

They finally pulled up at the bus station; "Take this envelope" Sir said with sharpness in his voice "$1000 should last you for a little while; you will be able to earn more money once to you get there. All money earned goes to Jackie; you will get your cut." "Yes sir, Minnie said as she jumped out the car to get her bus ticket".

Minnie dozed off waiting for the bus but was awaken when she hears the man on the speaker system' "Bus 754 for Florida leaving in twenty minutes", she grabs her things and head for the bus excited about seeing Kendra.

The bus ride was long and tiresome so Minnie decided to take a nap; she opened her eyes when the bus stopped and noticed a nice looking guy boarding the bus one hour and thirty minutes and into the ride. "So, where are you from missy?" He asked. Minnie didn't know whether to converse with this man or remain silent, "Cat got your tongue?" he laughed. Sir always told her to trust no one but him, the older she get she feel that Sir cannot be trusted either. "I am from Alabama", Minnie said in a low voice. "Are you riding alone little lady?" Minnie nodded yes. "Tell you what. I don't know how far you are going but if anyone asks, you are with me. Maybe that will keep people from bothering you", he smiled and Minnie smiled back feeling trust in this man.

The bus pulled off again, they both rode in silence. Minnie put her headphones on, determined not to make conversation with the stranger.

Three hours later the bus made a twenty minute stop over at the lower end of Alabama, four hours before Florida. The stranger told Minnie he was going to grab something to eat and if she wanted anything back, Minnie didn't want to leave the bus so she accepted his kind offer, "I'll just take a sandwich and a can soda". Minnie wanted a can soda to make sure he didn't try to slip anything in her drink; she saw that in a movie. "Oh, by the way..... My name is Paul if that makes you feel a little easier around me", he smiled and left the bus.

Paul returned with two sodas and two sandwiches, he handed Minnie hers and sat in the seat beside her. They still had ten minutes before the bus pulled out; Minnie got up to use the bathroom on the bus. She thought about getting off the bus to go the bathroom but the thought of the bus leaving her, Sir would never forgive her. There were only two other people on the bus besides she and Paul. When she opened the bathroom door to come out, Paul was standing there waiting. "I'm sorry I took too long; you can go in", Minnie said.

Paul pushed Minnie back in the bathroom and locked the door. Minnie had a reputation in Alabama and Paul knew exactly who she was when he first got on the bus. "Do you know who I am?" he asked. "I'm Sir's worst nightmare! I want you to deliver a message to your boss." He whispered the message in her ear; Minnie cringed and shook with fear

Paul exited the bathroom. Minnie paused a few minutes, peeped out the door and was very happy to see that he had left the bus. She was straightening herself up when she noticed he had dropped fifty dollars on the floor before leaving her in the bathroom. She slid back in the, closed the door, pulled out her cellphone and called Sir to tell him about her encounter with this man. Of course that was not his real name but she gave a very good description of him. Sir grunted, "I'll take care of this problem." She hung up the phone and went back to her seat.

chapter 5

Kendra was having the time of her life; she was so happy to be living with Jackie. They went shopping, to the movies and hung out at the beach almost every day since she got there. Jackie didn't work so they both shared all chores. She really enjoyed having Kendra around and was getting real attached to her as a little sister. "Hey Jackie, have you heard anything else from Minnie?" Jackie told her that Minnie will be here very soon and that they will be headed to the bus station to pick her up shortly, she did not care too much for Minnie and she made sure Minnie knew it.

Kendra and Jackie arrived at the bus station thirty minutes late, Minnie was furious. In Minnie's mind, Jackie arrived late on purpose. Kendra ran and gave her a big hug and started telling her all the things she and Jackie did and the places she'd seen. Minnie frowned a little; Jackie never took her anywhere fun or acknowledged her in any way other than a worker for Sir. "Girl, I am so glad you had fun and I knew Jackie would look out for you." "Hey Kendra, next week we're going to really have some fun." Jackie said as she looked at Minnie. Minnie knew exactly what Jackie was talking about; she knew to keep her mouth closed after her last encounter with Sir.

When they arrived at the house, Kendra helped Minnie get her bags and things out of the car. Jackie pulled her over to the side,

"Minnie, you know Sir has a lot of plans for your friend and you are responsible for making sure she follows all instructions." Minnie really did not like Jackie at all, she never treated her the way she treated Kendra. She never took her to the beach or to the movies; their relationship was always work. "I am going upstairs to call Sir to let him know you made it and get instructions on the plans and when to start. I figure give her until the rest of this week to get her primed up, Jackie said."

Sir picks up the phone on the first ring, anxious about his new found investment, "Hello Jackie, how is everything going down there? Did she adjust well or do we have a problem?" Jackie told Sir that all is well and she is going to wait until the end of the week to show her the ropes. "Start with something simple but make sure you get what you need so when the time is right, you'll have her eating out of your hands. Get Minnie, I need to speak with her immediately."

Minnie bounces upstairs to the phone and answers, "Yes Sir?" "Minnie, there's a lot of heat around here. Everyone is looking for this girl, there are posters everywhere and she is all over the news. It would have been better if you could have picked someone that the world wouldn't miss!" "She can never return home, you know that right? I can't take the risk of anyone getting caught, including me." "Your friend Josh, where does he live; I think I need to pay him a visit."

Minnie tried to convince Sir that Josh was cool even though he was not. She knew if the cops were to put a make on his car being in Kendra's drive way the day she became missing, he would squeal like a rat. "I'll call him if you want me too," there was no response from Sir. Minnie knew this was not good; Sir is going to make a visit to Josh one way or another. She gave him the address and information on the kind of car he drives.

chapter 6

Josh pulled in his driveway, just coming home from the movie. Just as he opened the front door, a car pulled in front of the house, "Hi Josh, may I have a word with you?" Josh feared he was with the police so he let Sir in to talk. As the conversation went on, he knew something was wrong.

"Who are you?" Josh asked. "What matter is that I know who you are," Sir said with a smirk on his face. I'm here to make you an offer. Your friend Minnie works for me, I understand she used your car to take care of something for me." Josh knew what and who Sir was talking about and knew exactly who Sir was. Minnie spoke of Sir so much; Josh knew everything about him and knew he was in danger.

"Before anyone comes looking for you to ask questions; and eventually they will; I am going to give you $5000. I want you to use this money to get your car painted, get rid of that license tag and get a new one. Once that is done; I will give you $2000 more to keep your mouth closed. I am planning on tripling my investment and then some." Sir got in the car and made a call, he gave the person on the other end the address where Josh lives and instructed him to follow Josh for a few days.

Josh was very afraid. He took the offer and with a handshake Sir walked to the door, turned, looked at Josh and said, "A handshake is like a contract you know. Don't break our contract." Josh knew exactly what he was trying to say, nodded his head and closed the door. First thing in the morning, Josh will drop the car off and fulfill his end of the contract.

Around noon the next day Josh drove his car to the paint and body shop downtown and instructed them to paint his car a golden mustard color with a black stripe. They told him it will be 2 weeks before he get the car back, he paid for it in cash and walked down the block to grab something to eat before going home.

Nicole was at the café when Josh walked in; he met up with some of his friends and ordered some food. She couldn't help but over hear the conversation when one of his friends started talking about the missing girl all over the news. Josh looked extremely nervous and started sweating. "Hey man, you alright?" one of his friends asked. "I got to go, I'm not feeling well." He left money on the table for the food he ordered and left out the door to catch the bus, Nicole followed him.

She walked to the back of the bus and watched Josh's reaction as he looked at the newspaper the old man across from him was reading. On the front page was a picture of the missing girl. Beads of sweat were forming on his face and sweat was running down his back.

When Josh stepped off the bus, Nicole followed him. She did not see the stranger following them; the only thing on her mind was to ask Josh some questions. As Josh began to walk up the drive way, Nicole touched his shoulder. "Excuse me, I saw you in the café earlier and overheard your friends talking about the missing girl. Do you or any of your friends know her? Have you seen her?" Josh gave her a long bland stare before answering no. "I've been posting up pictures all over town and talking to everyone I know. Please, look at this picture again. Have you seen my daughter?" Again Josh answer no. Nicole noticed how nervous he was acting and how sweaty he became from the conversation. "If you see or hear anything; please contact the police for me." Josh shook his head and went inside the house.

The stranger makes a call to Sir. "The young boy dropped his car off at the paint and body shop and went to the café. There was conversation between him and his friends about a missing girl. The boy was looking nervous and left, he caught the bus to his house. There was a lady there too, she followed him and got on the same bus. When he got off at his stop, so did she. They talked to him for about fifteen minutes; she showed him a piece of paper then left. Right now he is home; I don't think he will be leaving out anymore tonight." Sir told him that was great information and that he will not be needing him to follow Josh anymore, "I will wire some money in the account tonight." He hangs up.

Josh took a shower and was sitting on the sofa watching television, seeing the face of the little girl was really getting to him, he was awaken by a knock on the door. He was shocked to see Sir standing there when he opened it, he begin to speak immediately. "Josh, I was informed that someone was asking you questions today. I was also informed that the lady followed you home, who was she?" Josh could not answer the question; he didn't know the lady but he knew what she wanted. Josh told Sir that she was asking questions about the little missing girl. "So what caused her to follow you home and ask questions? Did you do or say something? Does she know you?" Josh told Sir he had never seen nor spoken to her and that he had handled the situation. Sir smiled at Josh, shook his hand and left.

chapter 7

Around two o'clock AM a tall figure strolled through the night, walked around the side of Josh's house and disappeared in through a window down stairs that was left slightly open. Josh lay asleep on the sofa and did not see or feel his death coming as a sharp knife went across his throat, he breathed his last breath. The intruder left out the front door, walked to the end of the driveway, stopped and looked up the street to the left. Sir was sitting in the car a few blocks away, the stranger lit a lighter one time and disappeared into the night, Sir drove away.

Nicole is up early, moving slowly around the house from a restless night. She thought about the guy from the café and how nervous he reacted to seeing her daughters face on the flyer she showed him. Nicole couldn't get it out of her head, "He was so nervous, he really looked spooked. I have to go talk to him again, he knows something and I am going to find out." She took a shower went downstairs to get some coffee, when she turned on the television she got the shock of her life. "THE BODY OF JOSH AVERY WAS FOUND DEAD IN HIS HOME, THERE IS NO ESTIMATED TIME OF DEATH. INVESTIGATORS ARE CURRENTLY ON THE SCENE LOOKING FOR CLUES TO THIS GRUESOME MURDER. STAY TUNED FOR MORE DETAILS AROUND NOON." Nicole calls the police.

The cops showed up at Nicole's house around eleven o'clock, she tells them everything that happened from the café to the conversation she and Josh had after she followed him home. "So, where were you when the murder took place?" one of the cops asked. "I was home," Nicole stated as she looked curiously at the cop. "I know what you're getting at and no, I do not have an alibi!" "My daughter is missing and you think I murdered that boy!" "If I murdered him; why would I call you?" "Don't leave town," officer Ray stated forcefully they left the house.

Two of the guys Josh was talking to the day before were sitting in a booth at the back of the café talking about his death when they heard someone say, "So you knew Josh?" They looked up and saw 2 cops standing close by. The guy with the dark hair said yes and the shorter guy said no. Officer Ray took another step and asked, "Which is it?" The guy with the dark hair looked at his friend, nodded, looked at the cop and said "We've been friends since middle school, he was a great person; everyone liked him." The cops asked, "When was the last time they saw or talked to Josh". "We were together here at the café, he started and said he didn't feel good so he left." The cops asked if he look sick when he came in... "No" the shorter guy said "he was fine. We saw the news alert that there is a missing girl that lived in this town. You would almost think he knew her the way he was looking at the TV. He started sweating and looked pale ..... He left. I guess his family will be picking up his car." Officer Ray looked puzzled, "Where is his car?" They pointed towards the paint and body shop. "Don't leave town," office Ray said. Both cops turned and left the café. "Let's go see this car and find out how long it's been in the shop and why."

Pete was under the hood of a 57 Chevy when the cops walked in. "Nice car", stated officer Ray. Pete was very familiar with these cops and knew not to comment about anything unless asked but answer with little to no information. "Been keeping your nose clean Pete?" no answer. Pete stood there for a moment wondering what brought them his way; he knew there was nothing there that would get him into trouble with the law again unless he is being set up. "Listen, I don't know what you heard but I am clean." "I know you are", said Officer Ray. "We're here about the car that belonged to Josh Avery. Of course you know he was murdered last night and we're going to get a warrant to haul his car to the police impound. Can you show us the car?" Pete showed them the car; they wrote the tag and VIN number down. "Why did he bring the car in?" Ray asked with a puzzled look on his face. Pete told him that Josh brought the car in to get painted and paid cash for it. Ray and his partner gathered enough information to head downtown and get a warrant to impound the car.

At the station; Officer Ray had them run the VIN number to Josh's car. They got a warrant to check the house and the car and had agents on standby to process the car." I don't know if he have anything to do with the little girl's disappearance but we need to speed things up and find her as soon as possible. This has never happened in our town and I'm going to make sure it never happens again."

Nicole was already on her way to the police station when Officer Ray called her. "Hi Nicole, this is Officer Ray. Do you know anything about Josh and why you would even think he had something to do with your daughter's disappearance?" Nicole had never met Josh before the day in the café but her mother's instinct told her that even if Josh had nothing to personally do with it, he knew something about it. Now, he's not around to tell us what happened or where Kendra could possibly be. "No I don't, Nicole said. It's just that he looked very afraid when he saw my daughter's face on the TV screen and also when I showed him a picture of her after I followed him home. I just asked him a few questions, when I left he still looked pale but he was fine." Officer Ray wrote down a few more notes and hung up the phone.

chapter 8

Minnie couldn't get Josh off her mind, she would not dare ask Sir if he is okay. She dialed his number but did not get an answer, "Maybe he's out and about, I'll try again later." Minnie, Kendra and Jackie all sat around and talked about all the things Florida has to offer, pumped up with excitement they stayed up until midnight. Before Minnie went to bed; she tried calling Josh again, still no answer so she called a friend and asked if he had seen or heard from him. "You didn't hear? Josh is dead! Someone crawled in through the window while he was asleep. The cops are looking for the person who did it, they even impounded his car!" Minnie couldn't speak, her face was flushed. She knew Sir had something to do with Josh's murder; she lay on the bed and cried herself to sleep.

Jackie receives a call from Sir around one o'clock AM, "It's time to put her to work. It's getting too hot here, everyone is looking for her. It's just a matter of time before her face is floating all around town there; I need my investment to pay off. You know what to do." Jackie took a bag out of her closet and went downstairs while Minnie and Kendra slept in their rooms. Per Sir's instructions, she mixed together the ingredients that she would slowly give to Kendra. When she finished; she sat and thought of the good days they shared and started having second thoughts about Sir's plans. She also knew if she didn't follow his instruction, the same thing might happen to her that happened to Josh. "There's got to be another way, I have to get this innocent little girl back home to her mother.

Kendra tossed and turned as she dreamed of her mother smiling, laughing and hugging her. Minnie heard her crying in her sleep and calling her mom, she did not go in her room. Minnie knew all too well how she missed her mom when she ran away. "I'll be here for you," she whispered as the sound of sobbing from Kendra's room got less and less .... Kendra went back to sleep.

The next morning, Kendra and Minnie woke to the smell of breakfast. They ran downstairs and squealed, "Pancakes, bacon, eggs, sausage, fruit!" "I'm starving." Kendra said as she sat at the table, Jackie fixed her plate. She reached in the bag in the drawer and sprinkled some of the mixture on top of her pancakes; she topped the mixture with whipped cream. "A little at a time, I don't want to have her in a coma before night." Jackie said while passing Kendra her plate. Minnie saw what she did but dared say a word, she knew that later that night Kendra's world would change forever.

"Hey Kendra!" Minnie called from the kitchen "Don't you want to come help me in the kitchen? I wash you dry!" Minnie kept washing dishes but never received an answer. She called her again, no answer. She grabbed the towel, dried her hands and walked towards the den.

"Jackie! Jackie! Jackieeeeee!" Jackie came running down stairs; she had just stepped out of the shower when she heard the loud screams of her name. Kendra lay on the floor, not moving but was breathing normal. Jackie told Minnie to help get her to the sofa; I'll call DOC. "Are we going to call Sir too?" "No" Jackie said as she fumbled through the drawer by the fireplace. DOC answered the phone on the first ring; he was on his way out the door when the phone rang. "I was headed in that direction anyway, be there in a few. Make sure you keep a watch on her and keep her head slightly elevated."

When DOC arrived, Kendra had regained consciousness a little. She did not recall passing out at all or how she got on the chair. DOC checked her out and smirked when finished, "Well well, it seems little miss missy is slightly clumsy. Looks like she forgot the little step down in the den; tripped and bumped her head. "Looks like she won't be going anywhere tonight," Jackie said. She headed upstairs to call Sir. "Plans for tonight have been changed, there was a little accident. Doc says Kendra will be okay; she just bumped her head a little. I think the dose I gave her was too strong, a little rest and she'll be good as new!" Sir did not like the news but he didn't have a choice.

"Well" sighed Minnie "Since we are not going out tonight; how about a movie?" Kendra was all smiles until Minnie said "Let's watch this one." Kendra face turned red while tears began streaming down her face. When Jackie came in the room, she looked at Kendra then at Minnie. "What did you say to her!" Jackie shouted in a very loud angry voice. Kendra told Jackie that she didn't say anything to her, it's the movie. "But it haven't started yet" Jackie said frowning. Kendra began telling them how it was her favorite movie and how she and her mom use to sit up and watch it on rainy days when there was nothing to do. She told them how they laughed so hard until they cried. Kendra really began to miss home. "I think I'll just go to bed, my head hurt." Neither said a thing, they all went to bed.

chapter 9

Ray decided to head over to the café for a bite to eat and hopefully stumble on some more information that would lead to Kendra's disappearance. His cell phone rings as he begins sipping his coffee. "Hey Ray, just wanted to let you know the warrant is ready and that you might want to pick it up before the chief leave for the day." "On the way," he dashed out the door.

Just as he arrived at the station and walked through the door; the chief came strolling out with his briefcase in his hand. "Glad I caught you Chief, I need to grab that warrant and head over to the shop to get that car towed before night." "It is night" the chief growled and began walking to his car. "I know my fine officers need to do their jobs but it would be nice if you could have made it here before my work day is over. I guess you are expecting me to go back in there and get it for you huh? Well Ray, you are wrong. I am headed home to my lovely wife and kids. I will be in at eight o'clock in the morning; I suggest you do the same." Ray really wanted the warrant tonight but he knew that was not about to happen. He decided to do a stakeout on the garage to make sure the car doesn't disappear overnight.

The shop closes at seven o'clock PM; Ray was there at six fifty-eight. He parked in an alley 'bout a half a block down from the shop but where he can easily see the front door to the shop. Around eight

PM his stomach began growling, he realized not only did he not have time to finish the food he ordered earlier from the café but he also did not pick up anything on the way. He also noticed that the lights were still on in the shop and no one exited the building. Around eight o'clock PM the door opens and out steps Pete and another gentleman. Ray could not see the man's face; he wore large dark shades, a hat pulled down to hide his face and his collar was flipped up to hide the lower part of his face. He never turned to face the direction where Ray was parked, the two men stood and talked a few more minutes. The unknown gentleman walked about a half a block up the street, got in a black Mercedes with dark tint on the windows and drove away in the opposite direction from were Ray was parked. Pete's car was parked in the front of the building; he left headed in the opposite direction as well.

Ray's cell phone rang around nine-thirty pm, "Hey Ray! How's things going? I stopped by your house but no one was home …. What else is new!" the voice on the other end yelled and began laughing. "Frank! Thinking of old ghosts! I am great but really hungry; can you grab some food for me? We can catch up when you get here." Ray gave Frank his location, "If anyone asks about me; you haven't talked to me." Frank agreed to Rays demands and arrived with the food around ten o'clock PM. He hopped in the car with Ray and immediately Ray started devouring his food. "Slow down man, you act like you haven't had a meal in days; and why are we sitting in a parked car in this alley?" "Ray laughed; man I've been so busy today I haven't had time to eat." Ray began telling Frank that he was doing an unauthorized stakeout that may have something to do with the disappearance of the little girl on the news and that he couldn't tell him anything else right now. They sat, talked and laughed about the good ole days and of the many unauthorized stakeouts they've had together until they both dozed off.

Frank opened his eyes around three o'clock AM, "Ray! Ray! The shop across the street is on fire!" Ray told Frank to dial 911; Ray jumped out of the car and started to run across the street when he noticed a tall dark stranger running from the building. He knew he didn't have time to chase him; he had to get the car and all possible evidence out of the shop. Frank came towards Ray, they are on the way. "Frank! I have a warrant for that car sitting right there!" he said pointing to the window. "I have to save that car! I have to get it out of there!"

Frank ran to the side of the building, broke a small window and entered the building and opened the shops front door. He and Ray pushed the car out of the shop towards the alley where Ray's car was parked, the fire trucks arrived less than a minute later. The fire didn't cause a lot of damage but there was enough damage to know that Pete was going to be very upset. Ray called the towing company to have the car towed to a safer place and also knew he would have to deal with the chief in the morning.

The cops and fire department arrived at the same time; Pete had arrived to the scene as well. Frank and Ray were already talking to one of the officers when Pete walked up looking very puzzled. They officer and one of the fire fighters told him that the fire started in the office and because this is an old building the fire didn't spread fast because it is made out of brick throughout. "Whoever started this fire didn't know about that huh?" the police officer stated. "Where is the car? There was a 2000 Chevy Impala inside when I closed shop for the day?" Pete said frantically. The fire fighter told him there was no Chevy Impala in the shop, just the jeep sitting there on a jack with two tires missing, no damage there either. "I was driving by and saw the fire. I have a warrant to get that car in the morning; it's for a very important case. The car is safe and sound, you can check with the chief if you'd like." Ray stated. The other officer contacted the chief who was also not happy at all about being awaken at four thirty in the morning. Once the fire was taking care of and the damage was written up; Ray and Frank went to talk to Pete. "You don't seem upset at all about the damage to your shop; you look like you are afraid of something. Is everything ok? And who was the guy you were talking to outside the shop before you left? I've never seen him before." Ray questioned. "Look Officer Ray" Pete said wearily "I am very tired right now, maybe later in the afternoon. Here is my address; I'll be home around two thirty."

chapter 10

Kendra tossed and turned all night, Minnie could hear her from her room. Jackie had breakfast done, "This time I will give her a smaller dose." The girls came down stairs looking tired and down, "We need a little picker upper in this house! How about after breakfast we head out to do some shopping and hit the beach for the day?" Minnie could not believe her ears, she have known Jackie for years and she has never taken her shopping or to the beach. When she was sent to Florida, Jackie put her straight to work; she was beginning to really envy Kendra. "I need to turn Jackie against Kendra, or maybe the other way around. Either one works for me but I need Jackie to think that Kendra is not as good as she think she is but for the day I am going to enjoy all the shopping and the day at the beach." Jackie made everyone some quick smoothies, "Just a little extra something in Kendra's for tonight and we're off."

They jumped in Jackie's car and headed to town, the main strip was always moving. "I don't think this place ever sleeps." Jackie said. Here we are, let's get this day started! We will start with a little shopping, grab some beach wear and hit the beach for a few hours." They girls were very excited, especially Minnie, she was going to enjoy this treat and try to get on Jackie's good side for a change even if it meant helping her get Kendra where Sir wanted her.

They walked in a very nice clothing store loaded for beautiful dresses, pants, lots of hats and accessories "Ok girls listen. You are allowed to pick two outfits with accessories for both, let's see what kind of taste you two have. There are some nice bathing suits over there too; we are going to turn some heads at the beach." They all laughed and hit the racks. The outfits both girls picked out were okay but neither outfit was suitable to wear tonight. Jackie told them that she would pick out one special item for the both of them, and she did but she did not let them see it. She said it was a surprise.

After shopping they grabbed something to nibble on, some cool drinks and decided to hit the beach. They changed in the dressing room at the beach and enjoyed a few hours walking around, turning heads and flirting. "This is so much fun!" Kendra shouted "but I am a little hungry now." They wrapped the towels around them, got their clothes from the lockers and went to find something to eat. "Hey girls, I have a super idea. Since we're already out and miles away from home; why don't we just get a room here and relax? I mean, what are we rushing home for? I'll go get a room, you two get the bags but do not look in the surprise bag or else." Kendra laughed but Minnie just smiled, she knew Jackie was very serious. To the car they went, Kendra turned to look at Jackie with a curious look.

While they were gone, Jackie called Sir. He asked if she did everything he told her to do today, she said yes. They stayed on the phone for the entire time the girls were gone, when she saw them coming she hung up. "Got the room! Let's get this stuff up there, get changed and head out to grab a bite to eat. How are you feeling Kendra? Is your head okay?" Kendra assured both that she was feeling great but her head still hurts just a little. Jackie hands her a little capsule for her headache, "Let's get some food now."

The food was great; they headed back to the room. Kendra was alert with lots of energy; Minnie could tell something was different about her. When they got back to the room; Jackie showed both of them the outfits she picked out for them earlier. Kendra grabbed hers and began to dance around the room, laughing and singing. "Jackie, I know you talked to Sir earlier and I know these outfits have something to do with tonight." Jackie filled her in on what was going to happen tonight, she helped her get Minnie cleaned up and dressed. Once they finished getting ready they all headed out to this little spot for dancing; no one questioned the girls ages ...... the lounge belonged to Sir.

They sat at a table close to the front; Kendra got up and started to dance. By now; she have had three small doses of Jackie's mixture, was very alert and feeling really good. "Look at her dance! That lace looks great on her too," One of the guys shouted. Jackie made an announcement, "Okay guys; meet our newest addition to the family! Here's Sweetness! One Hundred Dollars and you can dance with her. No grabbing; you can hold her close to you and dance any way you like. Anyone that would like to dance with her, come on up!" About twenty men went to the front, Jackie collected their money and they all took turns dancing with Kendra. They passed her from person to person as the slow music played. She was unaware of her actions, only knew she was having the time of her life as they were slow dancing and grinding on her. This generated more money for Sir's club, these men were so turned on they paid extra money to go to the back room with the more experienced women for unlimited pleasure. Jackie collected over $2000 for Kendra's performance tonight, she was tired and they headed back to the room. Minnie helped Jackie get her cleaned up and ready for bed, she went straight to sleep.

The next morning Kendra was up early, smiling and singing around the room. "Wow, I feel great! I don't remember anything but I feel like I had the time of my life." Jackie laughed, "We all did and there's more to come tonight but right now we need to get packed up so we can be out of here at checkout." Kendra was excited about her night out with the girls again, Jackie showed them some beach wear she picked up for them for tonight, "I love it!" Kendra squealed "Are we going to the beach again today?" Jackie told her that they are going to a beach party tonight. "Hey Jackie? Where is Minnie's suit?" Jackie told Kendra that Minnie was not going to be able to come with them because she was invited to something else. Minnie's face went pale but she smiled at Kendra and said, "I'm sure to have fun too," then she looked at Jackie and rolled her eyes. Kendra went to shower and try on her suit.

"Jackie? Why I can't hang out with you two tonight?" Jackie told her that Sir had other plans for her tonight. She explained that Sir has some special business associates coming in town tonight and she will need to entertain them. She showed Minnie the dress Sir sent for this special occasion, looking at the dress; Minnie knew what kind of night this was going to be. "I thought I could have a break," Kendra said with tears in her eyes." "A break?!" Jackie snapped "And when have you ever had a break? When Sir makes money, I make my money so you're going to do exactly what you are told when you are told and how you are told to do it!"

chapter 11

Ray is at the station at seven forty five AM waiting on the chief, "He said be here when he get here so here I am. There will be no excuse this time for not getting the warrant today." The chief pulls up around eight-fifteen am; "You're late," Ray said with a grin. "Don't push your luck," the chief said frowning at Ray "come in my office; we have a lot to talk about." Ray sits down "So, you conveniently just happen to be driving by the garage last night around the same time the building just so happen to be on fire huh? Is there anything else you want to inform me?" Ray told the chief that he has reason to believe that there may be evidence in the car that might lead to Kendra's whereabouts or at least point them in the direction of someone who was in the car with her. "Honestly chief, I was parked in the alley about a half a block down waiting until morning. I woke up around three o'clock AM and the building was on fire so I ran around to the side of the building to a small window and broke it to get in. Another guy was driving by and stopped to help me push the car out after I got the garage door open." The chief nodded his head and said "No one issued a stakeout on the shop did they. And where is the car now?" It's safe, waiting to be towed in for processing after I bring them the warrant." The chief gave Ray the warrant; he stands, turns, looks back at the chief and said. "I would also like a warrant to question Pete, the shop owner." The chief look very puzzled. "I don't understand why you would want a warrant to question Pete. Don't you think he's been through enough being awaken early in the morning with a call that all that he worked for was on fire?" "There was not that much damage chief and besides; I have good reasons." "Well" said the chief "I'm listening". Ray told the chief what time he pulled up in the alley and that he saw Pete and an unknown man exit the building around eight o'clock PM or so. "They talked for a few minutes and the unknown man walked in the opposite direction. I could not follow him because I didn't want to leave my post." "And that is enough to get you a warrant to question him?" the chief said with a smirk? "No but after the building caught fire and before I ran across the street; I saw another guy running from the scene. This was a different person; the man leaving the fire was a taller, more slender male. I couldn't see his face; he was wearing all black and had on black gloves and shades. He ran off down the block and jumped in a black car with no tags. I have reason to believe Pete may have something to do with his garage being almost destroyed because he didn't look like a man who would normally be upset to loose or almost loose his shop. He looked like he was upset because it was saved." The chief issued the warrant for Ray to have Pete picked up and brought to the station for questioning.

Ray left the office with the warrant for the car when his cell phone rang, "Hey Ray; it's Nicole. Can you meet me at the café in an hour?" "Ok, I'll be there. I might be running a little late; I need to make a stop first." Nicole said okay and hung up the phone. Ray smiled at the thought of seeing Nicole again. Although his first mind is to find her daughter; his second mind wants to get to know Nicole. He has a lot of admiration for her, her determination to find her daughter at whatever cost. Most people just let the cops handle it, but not Nicole. "Maybe once all this is over and her daughter is found and brought home; I'll ask her out," He smiled again and headed to the garage to show them the warrant and have the car towed in for processing.

Nicole is sitting at a small booth in the back of the café; Ray immediately noticed her when he walked in. Nicole spoke to him, they ordered something to drink and eat and talked briefly about what happened from the time he parked by the shop to him finally getting the warrant. "Wait! I remember seeing a guy dressed in all black when I got on the bus and followed Josh home that night he was murdered. After I followed him off the bus at his stop, Josh and I talked outside his house but not long. He said he didn't feel well and needed to go lay down. I knew I didn't have too much time to talk to him; the last bus would be coming in twenty minutes. We talked the entire twenty minutes or so and I walked back to the bus stop and waited. I looked down the block and saw a man just standing there smoking a cigarette by a dark colored car. When the bus pulled up; I got on and it passed right by him. I looked at him when the bus passed by and I could swear it looked like he was looking right at me. I turned and looked back and it looked like his head was turned in the opposite direction up the street in the direction of Josh's house but again; it was dark and late at night. Ray asked her if there was anything else she could remember about that night or about the evening her daughter disappeared but that was it.

They finished eating lunch and talked for a little while longer. "Oh! I need to head back to the station to get the warrant to talk to Pete before the chief change his mind!" he laughed. "I call you later, ok?" Nicole smiled and nodded her head. He could almost say she winked at him but he was sure that was his mind playing tricks on him. "Damn! I think I'm falling for her. This is not the right time!" he cursed at himself and headed back to the station.

Ray walks in the station to get the warrant but the chief had already left. "He stepped out for a few, been gone for about two hours so he should be back shortly," his secretary said in a dry tone. "I'll wait." Ray replied back "I'm not waiting until tomorrow to have to get this warrant like the last one." He must have waited another hour before the chief walked back in, they spoke and the chief called him into the office. "I had to run a few errands but I have your warrant ready." The chief handed him the warrant and he hurriedly left the office with a uniformed cop following him to bring Pete in for questioning.

They arrived at Pete's house thirty minutes later and knocked on the door, no answer. Ray calls him on the phone, still no answer. The uniformed cop walks around to the back of the house and peeps in through the back door window to find Pete lying faced down on the floor in a pool of blood. "I found him!" yells the unformed cop. Ray run to the back of the house, "I just talked to him early this morning. He was looking nervous and said he wanted me to meet him at his house today. I wanted to get a warrant and bring him in so that nothing he says is compromised; now he's dead and everything he wanted to say is gone with him. Ray held his head down and cursed at himself; I should have just come over and talked to him.

Ray notice Pete's left hand was balled up, he looked around for the uniformed officer who had went outside to tape off the yard. He grabbed a towel from the kitchen counter, pried Pete's hand open and removed the paper. The note read 'PHONE 7733', "was he trying to jot down a phone number?" Ray sat puzzled for a minute and figured he was either referring to his cell phone or home phone so he tried calling Pete's cell phone, no answer."Whoever killed Pete must have taken his cell phone." He walked over to the home phone; the answering machine light was blinking. Ray pushed the button on the answering machine, it asked for a code so he entered 7733. There were three messages; the first from some lady about a bill, the second was from someone who's car Pete had previously worked on 'the car broke down, asking if have time to come out to the house to check on it.'

The third message stunned Ray .... "I was told that you were being questioned this morning about the fire and about talking to me. I am sending someone over to give you a package so pack whatever you can to leave town," the voice on the answering machine whispered. Ray could not recognize the voice, "I am sure the person that was sent over killed Pete.

The officer came back in the house when the crime lab tech arrived to collect evidence and take the body back for processing. "We'll let you know what we find Ray," they said as they took the body out.

Walking back to his car; Ray thought about the message on the answering machine and wondered who the man could be the other end. He sat in his car still cursing himself for not talking to Pete earlier when his cell phone rang, "Hey Ray, it's Frank. I just heard over the radio that Pete was found dead in his home! What happened? Do you know anything yet?" Ray told him about the paper balled up in his hand with the code to the answering machine, that Pete's cell phone was missing and about the message that was on the answering machine. "I couldn't recognize the voice but I know that Josh's death was related to Pete's."

After he hung up with Frank he called the chief and told him that the warrant is no longer needed because Pete is dead. "He was found on the kitchen floor in a pool of blood, the crime team is taking the body in for processing now." The chief told Ray that he will call the crime lab and make sure all evidence is tagged and turned over to him as soon as possible. Ray thanked him and started his car.

chapter 12

"Hello? Okay, I'm on the way. Ray is anxious while driving to the vehicle processing department, "At least I was able to salvage something out of this case." He arrived there in thirty-five minutes; they waited on him before they started. He pulled up a chair and looked over the notes while he waited to see whatever evidence the lab team could retrieve from the car. It took them three hours to process the car; they collected evidence from the inside of the car to the dirt on the tires on the outside of the car. "Here is a list of all items collected from the inside of the car:

1. Lip gloss
2. Nail file
3. A receipt from Pete's garage for the service to be done to the car and the amount Josh paid in full to him.
4. A girls hat
5. Chewed gum wrapped in foil

"We found a few strands of hair in the hat and we're sending the gum into the lab to run the DNA from the saliva against anyone that may already be in the system." They bagged and tagged all items and sent them all to the lab, Ray was sure not to touch anything to insure none of the evidence was compromised. "I need to call Nicole, please answer!"

Nicole answers on the first ring as if she was waiting on Ray to call, he swear he could hear her smiling through the phone. "Hello? Yes I am home. I'll be here when you get here." Ray headed over to Nicole's, for the first time since he started investigating Kendra's disappearance he was feeling good. "Please have what I am looking for Nicole!" Ray said with excitement.

He pulled in front of Nicole's house, got out of the car and briskly walked to the door. Nicole was looking out the window waiting on him; she opened the door immediately as he pulled up. "What's going on that you needed to come to the house? Did you find anything new?" "I'm not sure just yet but I have a good feeling right now about the evidence they pulled from the car so I need a few things from you so the crime lab can run the DNA test. Do you happen to have a comb or brush with your daughter's hair in it and maybe a toothbrush or something that she always puts in her mouth?" Nicole gave Ray Kendra's hair brush and toothbrush, "She always kept her stuff in my bathroom so I'm sure that's why she forgot to take it with her but what's going on Ray?" "I can't tell you yet but I will let you know when we get the results back from the crime lab," Ray said. "We're going to find her Nicole." She gave him a big hug and told him thank you. He headed straight to the lab so they could run a match against the evidence they found in the car.

Ray met up with Frank; they sit and discuss everything that went on from the beginning of the stakeout until now. "It took how long for the chief to return back to the station?" Frank asked with a puzzled look on his face. "He never leaves the building for a long period of time. You know his motto......'THE CAPTIAN CANNOT RUN THE SHIP IF HE'S NOT ON BOARD!' They both laughed as they have both heard the chief say it for so many years. "Maybe he had a family emergency or something, all I know is; I got there too late. Maybe I should have talked to him first before I took the impound yard the warrant for the car. Not like the car was going anywhere but with the way things been going lately; the car would have disappeared too huh?"

(Ray's cell phone rings) ...... 'Hi Ray, this is the lab. You need to get in here as soon as possible.' "Frank, I need to get to the lab. We will definitely catch up later, be careful and watch your back for anyone suspicious. I haven't told anyone that you were with me the night of the fire or that I've been talking to you on the phone so you should be okay; just be careful Frank." "You too," Frank said before parting ways.

When Ray arrived at the lab; they passed him an envelope, he carefully opened it. After reading that the results of the items brought in matched to what was found in the car; he immediately called Nicole while heading to the chiefs office with the good news. "Nicole! Hey listen. I know you have to work tonight but I have a lead on your daughter that I need to discuss. I do not want you to discuss any conversation we have with anyone; can you do that for me?" I will call you right after I talk to the chief." Nicole was so excited; she couldn't get her normal nap in before heading to the hospital for her twelve hour shift.

The chief was sitting at his desk on the phone when Ray knocked once and walked in; the door was pushed up but not closed. "Oh, I apologize. The door was not closed all the way like it normally is when you're on the phone," Ray said smiling. "I'll call you back in a few," the chief said to the person on the line. "I apologize chief but we have a break-through. The gum from the car matched the saliva from Kendra's toothbrush we retrieved from her home; she was definitely in Josh's car. I remember questioning him; he said he'd never seen her. Nicole's mom asked Josh about her too and was told the same thing yet her saliva was found in his car. Josh is not around to say anything but maybe if we could find the other girl" the chief cut him off ..... "Other girl? What other girl?" Ray began to speak again "The lab found hair in a hat that was left in the car. They ran it against the hair from Kendra's brush but there was not match but when they ran it through the system they came up with a match. The hair belongs to a missing teen names Sarah Tooles; she's been missing for a while. I have a printout with her photo; I think I'll check around town to see if anyone knows her too." Ray leaves the office whistling.

Ray sets up an interview with the news in hopes that someone would come forward with answers to the whereabouts of Kendra and Sarah Tooles. Well, at least Kendra for now until he can gather more information on Sarah.

BREAKING NEWS

THE POLICE HAVE IMPOUNDED THE CAR OF JOSH FITZ AND FOUND EVIDENCE THAT LINKED HIM TO THE MISSING TEEN 'KENDRA' TO BEING IN HIS CAR BEFORE HER DISAPPEARANCE. JOSH WAS FOUND DEAD IN HIS HOME 3 WEEKS AGO. KENDRA MAY HAVE BEEN LAST SEEN IN A 2002 CHEVY IMPALA AND MAY HAVE BEEN ACCOMPANIED BY ANOTHER MISSING TEEN 'SARAH TOOLE'. IF ANYONE HAS SEEN EITHER OF THESE TWO GIRLS; PLEASE CONTACT THE POLICE AT 555-555-5555.

chapter 13

Minnie walks outside to make a few calls back home. "Hey, this is Minnie. Just checking to see how things were going back home; did they ever find that missing girl?" The voice on the other end of the receiver tells her that there was another death around town and starts informing her of everything that is going on...... "It's crazy around here girl! This town has gotten sooooo unreal! First they found Josh dead and impounded his car, they found his car at Pete's garage and impounded it so I am sure the cops have it right now probably looking for some kind of clues; maybe they could find who killed him or something. Then the craziest thing! Pete turned up dead in his home! They say he committed suicide! Then it was something on the news about linking Josh to the missing girl and someone named Sarah Toole, they say she is another missing teen. I don't know her but I hope they find both of them." Minnie didn't say anything for a minute but the voice on the other end could hear her breathing, "Did you hear what I said girl?" "Yeah" Minnie said in a low voice "I heard you. Look, I got something to do. I'll call you back later. I might need a favor too. And if anyone asks; you don't know where I am and have not talked to me. You hear me? Do you hear me!?" The voice on the other end yells "YES I HEAR YOU AND SO DO CHINA! I got you girl."

Minnie sat on the steps of the porch trying to think, "Did we leave anything in the car? Think Minnie think! Ugggghhhhh! If Sir wasn't rushing me I would have been a little more careful. I was careful, I know I was or Sir would have called me by now. Or had he called? I need to talk to Jackie, if he called anyone it would be her."

As she walked into the house; Minnie hears Jackie in the kitchen. "Who is she talking to? I didn't see anyone come in, maybe they came in through the back." She looked around for Kendra downstairs, "Hummm, she must be in her room." Minnie is headed for her room but stops when she hears sobbing coming from Kendra's bedroom, the door is cracked open. She tips over to peep in to make sure Kendra is okay and sees her crying and looking at something. KNOCK! KNOCK! Kendra jumps and shoves something under a pillow. "Hey girl, are you okay?" Minnie asked while trying to peep to see what she was looking at when she heard her crying. "I was headed to my room and I heard you crying." "Please don't tell Jackie" Kendra whispered "I asked her if I could borrow her phone to call my mom just to hear her voice but she said no, she let me borrow it before. I never say anything because I don't know what to say. I am having fun but I really miss my mom. Minnie, I want to go home."

Minnie looked at Kendra for a second then said, "Let me go talk to Jackie, I think we need to have a teenage girls night out. We won't stay out too late, Jackie wouldn't allow that but, you will definitely remember everything we do. Stop crying and clean your face up before Jackie sees you, trust me." Kendra gave Minnie a puzzled look and went into the bathroom to freshen up. "Why did that statement not sound right?" She thought while wiping her face with a cold wet cloth.

Jackie is still on the phone when Minnie returns back downstairs, "Oh! I didn't know you were still on the phone. I came in earlier and you were on the phone so I went upstairs, I figured you'd be off by now."

"Yes. Ok. Yes. I'll take care of it." Jackie hangs up the phone, turns in Minnie's direction. "It's okay I was getting off the phone anyway, there has been a change of plans for tonight. I will not be taking Kendra to the pool party tonight; I have something to do so I want you to entertain her for me." Is this pure luck or was Jackie listening to our conversation earlier? "Uh? Sure? But I don't have any money." Jackie told her that she will give them some money and that she will probably be in late tonight. "What's going on? Is everything ok?" Minnie asked. "Just do as I asked and stop asking questions!" Jackie snapped. Minnie smiled a little smirk; this would be her opportunity to talk to Kendra alone and try to gain her trust. "Jackie? Have you talked to Sir lately about anything going on back in Alabama?" Jackie took a step toward Minnie, "Let me tell you for the first and last time. My conversations with Sir are none of your business. When and what is said is none of your concern, do you understand me?" Minnie looked at Jackie with water in her eyes and shook her head yes.

"Okay, something is going on. "But what"? Kendra had already come downstairs and was sitting in the living room watching television when Minnie walked out of the kitchen. "Hey girl, good news!" she said with the biggest smile in the world. "Jackie said no pool party for you. "And how is that good news?" Kendra asked. Minnie plopped on the chair beside her "Well, Jackie said the two of us can hang out tonight. She's even going to give us some money, said she have something very important to do or something sooooo it's just the two of us." Kendra smiled.

chapter 14

Nicole sees the news and impatiently calls Ray. "Hello, Ray! Have you seen the news?" "Of course and I know all about it. As a matter of fact; that is what I needed to talk to you about. Do you have time to talk before work? I can be there in twenty minutes." Nicole would make time she thought as she told him yes.

Ray calls Frank to see if he'd heard anything else about the death of Josh and Pete and if anyone knows anything about the day Kendra went missing or about the other missing teen Sarah. "Ok, just keep poking around." He pulls up at Nicole's house around seven forty five PM; it has been two and a half weeks since Kendra disappeared. Before he can stop the car, she was already walking out the door towards him. Nicole was walking so fast, he could swear she was running. "Hi, let's go inside and talk." She pours them both a glass of tea while Ray was pulling papers out of his briefcase. "I'll get right to the point. The lab was able to find some evidence from Josh's car that would have, at some point, put Kendra in his car. Can you tell me if or how she would know him?" Nicole thought for a few minutes, "to be honest with you we've never met him before and I've never heard her mention him. She don't hang out, she's too young. She use to go to sleep overs but I took her there and picked her up. Why?" Ray told her that the lab found some chewed up gum that contained her saliva in the ashtray of Josh's car; he also told Nicole about the hair from the brush that belonged to a girl named Sarah Toole. "Another missing teen? I've never heard of her nor have I heard Kendra mention her. My daughter hardly ever talked about her friends, she was always mad because I gave her chores to do around here. We didn't have the best mother daughter relationship since her father died several years ago." Tears began to roll down her face. "Ray? Do you think my daughter is okay? Do you really think you can find her?" "I am going to do the best I can Nicole. In the meantime; if you hear or remember anything; call me immediately." Nicole stood to walk Ray to the door, she forced a smile before telling him "I will."

His phone rings while he is walking out to the car. "Yes Chief? No. There have been no more leads on either of the two missing teens or the death of Josh or Pete, all clues have gone cold but I am still on the case." The Chief told Ray that he has another case that he wants him to work on. "I know you have a lot going on with this case but they want the best of the best and specifically asked for you to handle it. I have all the information in my office, I have to leave town for a day or two so if I'm gone before you get here I'll leave it with my secretary." Ray headed over to the police station to catch the Chief before he leaves.

"HOW COULD I HAVE MISSED HIM ALREADY? HE CALLED ME 45 MINUTES AGO." RAY CALLED HIS PHONE BUT NOANSWER, HE LOOKS OVER THE PAPERWORK. "PETE? SOMEONE WANTS ME TO INVESTIGATE THE DEATH OF PETE BUT IT DOESN'T SAY WHO." HE TRIED CALLING THE CHIEF AGAIN, NO ANSWER. "WELL, GUESS I'LL GET STARTED ON THIS CASE BUT KENDRA'S MISSING CASE WILL BE MY NUMBER ONE PRIORITY!"

chapter 15

Jackie comes downstairs dressed in a sundress, wedged heels and her hair pulled back in a ponytail with a large sunhat and dark shades. Kendra stares at her before saying. "I have never seen you dress like this, a little dressed down for you." Jackie did not laugh or smile at the comment. "My father called and wanted me to meet with someone for him. What time are you two leaving the house and where are y'all hanging out?" Minnie knew she was talking about Sir; Jackie was a runaway just like she was. Sir was everyone's daddy. "I thought we'd go to the amusement park on the beach then the arcade room down the block later on." Minnie responded. Jackie handed her $500, whatever you don't spend you better bring back." Jackie handed her a cell phone and told them to call her if they need to and to only use it to call her. She walked out the door, turned back and gave Minnie and evil glare that left both girls puzzled.

The girls caught the bus around six PM and headed to the amusement park, they bought bands so they could ride everything. Kendra and Minnie both said at the same time, "I have never had so much fun!" they both laughed and they ran to get a few slices of pizza. Minnie was looking at Kendra with a very serious stare; she stopped eating and asked "What's wrong?" Minnie told Kendra that she needs to tell her some things but she needs her to keep it between them and no one else. "Kendra, I know you haven't spoken to your mom in a while. When I knocked on your door this morning, I saw you crying and looking at something .... What was it?" A tear fell from Kendra's eye; she looked up and told her it was a picture of her mom. "You know you were not supposed to bring items like that with you but I understand and I will not tell Jackie." Both girls finished eating and sat looking out at the water before Kendra said, "Minnie, I want to go home."

Jackie calls Sir, "I am here." Sir instructed her to go to the bar and ask the bartender for a cell phone left for Lilly. The bartender handed her the cell phone, Sir told her that she will receive a call in the next fifteen minutes and for her to answer all questions and do whatever the person tells her to do. The waiter came over and Jackie ordered a fruity mixed drink, she was listening to the music and was becoming really relaxed when the cell phone retrieved from the bartender vibrated across the table. Jackie jumped and was quickly removed from her relaxed zone, "Hello?" The voice on the other end asked Jackie several questions and she replied, "They said they were going to the amusement park on the beach and they were also going to head to the arcade down the block." He also wanted to know what they were wearing and the cell phone number that she gave them to contact her. "Do you know exactly what's going on?" the voice on the other end asked. Jackie told him that Sir has informed her of some things but she try not to get involved, just do as she is told. She figured the less she knew the better. "Go home and pack up all belongings of both girls, wipe the house down to get rid of all fingerprints. Let me ask you something, how long have you been living in that house?" Jackie told him she's been living there for three and a half years. "Time to move", He said. "Contact Sir for you next location setup, get everything you need to take with you, pack their stuff and bring it to me once I call you. After all this is complete;

I want you to burn that house down." Jackie was puzzled but she knew to follow all instructions to the letter. She knew something bad was getting ready to happen but like she said, the less she knew the better.

Back at the beach, Minnie tells Kendra that she is going to help her get back home. "Kendra, I need for you to really trust me. Jackie is not who or what you think she is and neither am I. I am going to tell you some things that will make you very mad at me but I am trying to correct them now. You do not belong here or living this lifestyle and if I don't get you back home some terrible, irreversible things are going to happen to you. The reason I know is because the same thing happened to me, the only difference between you and I is that you have someone who really loves you and is waiting for you back home. Jackie told us not to use her phone for outside calls so use mine and call your mom." Kendra's eyes watered up as she quickly dialed the numbers to home .... No one answered. When the answering machine came on, Kendra was too afraid and ashamed to leave a message .... She hangs up. "I'm sorry." Minnie said as she hugged her while she cried "We will try again later but in the meantime we need to get you home. Jackie is out and will be gone for a while, we need to go the house and grab your stuff; we can use this money to get you back home." Minnie reached in her pocket where she had the money, "Oh NO! I lost the money! I must have dropped it when I pulled some out for the food." Minnie knew this would be bad to have to explain to Jackie, now she needs to come up with an idea to make some fast cash to get Kendra out of Florida.

Jackie called the girls to check on them before heading back to the house, Minnie was too afraid to answer the phone so Kendra did. "Hey Jackie"! Yes, we are having a ball. Okay, we will call you when we get ready to head home". Jackie used her GPS to pin point the girl's location and made a phone call.

Jackie's phone rings, it's Sir "We need to dump the package, it's getting too hot here and they've also put a real name to our other guest there. Clean the House now!" Jackie told him the location of the girls, Sir made a call.

"Kendra" Minnie said in a dry voice "I need to make some money real quick and all I need you to do is distract people. Last night was not fun, you were being prepped to be pimped tonight but Jackie had something else to do. You were brought down here to make some money for a man that I currently live with in Alabama that I call my father. I am a runaway Kendra, and I don't want you to end up like me. I'm sorry I lied to you and tricked you into coming here but right now I need you to trust me."

They headed back to the amusement park, Minnie explained to her that she was going to pick pocket some people but needed her to distract them by asking for directions. Kendra was very nervous but she knew this was the only way she was going to get home. "I can't believe this, seven dollars and some change? At this rate we will be out here all night and for the next few days. Look for someone who is spending a lot of money, when they pull out their wallet or open their purse we will know which one to get." A short man walked up to the concession stand to buy a hot dog, fries and a drink, Minnie's eyes stretched wide open when she say the amount of money he had in his wallet. Kendra saw her face and walked over to the man to ask for directions to the ticket booth, he placed his wallet in his back pocket when she walked up. As he was giving her directions to the nearest booth; she fainted. The short man shouted for help as he fanned her. Minnie stooped down to help him and purposely lost balance. She leaned over his back and put so much pressure on him he did not notice that she took his wallet. This was very easy to do considering it was sticking slightly out his back pocket. To play it all off; she continued on helping him until Kendra opened her eyes and lifted her head, she got up and he helped her to the nearest bench. Minnie walked in the opposite direction and headed out towards the beach, Kendra saw where she was headed and followed her. "STOP"! Someone stop her, she stole my wallet!" The girls began to run out of the amusement area down the block and ducked in the nearest alley, the short guy was a little pudgy and could not catch them nor did he see which direction they went.

chapter 16

Nicole had just left a patients room and was walking past the waiting area when she heard the television, the comment of the missing teens made her stop immediately. She stood frozen but did not turn around; tears swelled in her eyes so she headed to the bathroom to wash her face and try to get her self together. The nurse sitting at the nurse's station saw her and walked in the bathroom behind her. "Nicole, you are dealing with a lot with your daughter being missing and I know you said you have to work to keep from going crazy but I think you really need to go home and get some rest. What if she calls? Is someone there to answer the phone?" Nicole looked at her for a minute and told her that no one else is there and she's been getting these calls when she's not home, she hears breathing but no one says anything. "Look, go home. If it is her and she calls again tonight at least you'd be there to answer the phone." Nicole strained a brief smile, "You are right, thank you." She grabbed her things from her locker and went home.

When she got home she immediately checked the answering machine. Nicole could hear breathing and noise in the background ..... Screaming, laughter; sounds like things moving around but no voice. She smiled; her gut feeling told her that it was Kendra letting her know she was alright. "Come home baby" she said with tears streaming down her face. Clinging the cordless phone close to her heart; she sat on the sofa and fell asleep. Eight–Thirty AM the phone rings, she answers it on the first ring, "Hello? Oh Ray, how are you? I came home early last night to be close to the phone but when I arrived and checked the messages someone had called earlier but didn't say anything." Ray told her he wanted to listen to the message to see if he could pick something up from the background noises. "I'll be home all day," she said before hanging up the phone. Ray makes another call; the Chief is still not answering the phone so he leaves a message for him to call him back concerning the case of Pete's death.

Nicole started a pot of coffee and went upstairs to take her shower. She took the cordless phone with her just in case. She stood under the water and let the water run over her head and down her back lost in mind, she jumps and looses though when the phone rang. Ray was outside already! She dried off quickly, threw on some sweats and a t-shirt and went downstairs to answer the door. "The answering machine is right there. Would you like a cup of coffee?" Ray sat down and listened to the message and lost all thought when Nicole walked into the room, he had never seen her looking so beautiful. She handed him the coffee and asked if he could get anything out of the recording. "Nicole, can I take this with me? We have technology at the station that will separate the noises from the laughter and any talking in the background. Do you have another one?" She handed him the tape and popped another one in. "I'll let you know if I pick up anything." Ray left and headed down to the station.

Nicole started making new flyers to pass out, "I am not giving up on my daughter. I know she is out there and someone knows what happened to her." She delivered the flyers to several cab services and the local bus and train station, her goal was to get out early and hurry back home just in case she get another call.

Around three forty-five PM she returned home and found another missed call on her answering machine, this time there was no sound in the background. She played the message several times hoping to hear something but whoever was on the other end hung up when the answering machine came on. "I can't take this! I am calling in tonight and staying home, I will not miss another call!" Nicole grabbed something to eat out the fridge, grabbed a bottle of water and turned on the TV in the living room. Her head was throbbing so bad, she took to aspirin, laid on the sofa and took a nap.

chapter 17

Minnie and Kendra was out of breath, the man they lifted the wallet from was yelling out telling them he was going to have them arrested when he find them. They stayed squatted in the dark alley for about fifteen minutes, "I think he's gone," Minnie said as she ducked her head out from behind the mound of garbage. "Check to see how much we have because I'm not doing this again, we might get caught. What if someone saw us?" said Kendra. The girls slowly and started walking quickly in the opposite direction as they exited the dark alley. POW! POW! POW! Kendra ran as fast as she could as she witnessed Minnie falling to the ground. She saw a tall dark stranger standing on the opposite side of the street .... POW! POW! "He's shooting at me? Why is he shooting at me and why did this guy shoot Minnie?!" She stayed low behind cars, ran about a half a block and ducked into a crowded area. Kendra knew Minnie had been shot but did not know if she was still alive until she heard two more distant shots. The Tall Dark Stranger found them, shot Minnie, doubled back and shot her two more time to make sure she was dead. Everyone stared at Kendra as she walked through the crowd sobbing, she couldn't tell anyone what happened, she's a runaway. "What if they lock me up? The money, the phone! I can't call home now, how am I going to get home?" She walked and walked, constantly looking around for the

Tall Dark Stranger that shot Minnie and who is now after her. After minutes if walking; Kendra came upon a payphone so she took her chances of trying to call her mom collect one last time just in case something happened to her. She wanted to tell her mom that she was sorry and that she loves her "AS BIG AS THE MOON"! a saying her mom use to tell her when she was a little girl. There was no answer.

Kendra felt like she'd been walking for over an hour, her head and eyes hurt from crying so much. Hungry, tired and cold she stumbles upon an old abandoned car; she looked around to see if anyone is around, slowly crawled into the back seat of the car, locked the doors and cried herself to sleep. While sleeping; all she could hear is Minnie screaming as she is being shot several times …. She jumped up from this nightmare unaware that she had only been asleep two hours, "I want to go home" Kendra cried out softly "Mom, I am so sorry". It was around five o'clock AM before she dozed back off.

The sun was beaming through the windows when she woke up, she didn't have a watch so she was unaware of the time. She unlocked the door, crawled out of the car and looked around for a bathroom but did not see one so she ducked around the side of the building about a half block down. "I don't know where I am or which direction to begin walking in but I need to find something to eat and figure out a way to get home." Kendra saw the amusement park from a distance so she headed in that direction, it was too early for them to be open but she did see people moving around. She quickly ducked into an alley as she heard voices that sound like people were coming up behind her; she hid behind a large dumpster and jumped when she heard a door being pushed open and something being dumped in the dumpster.

After the door closed back and the voices passed the alley; she peeped out to make sure the coast was clear and climbed into the dumpster. "Food! He threw out food!" Kendra cringed at the thought of eating out of a dumpster but she felt right now she needs to eat to survive as she had nowhere else to turn. A half eaten piece of chicken, stale bread, old fries and a cold hard piece of pizza was the best meal she felt she had in her entire life. She tried not to think of where it was coming from as she ate it; all she knew was that it hit the spot. Feeling a little better; she decided to find someone to ask which direction is Alabama.

Kendra walked into a convenience store and told the clerk that her mom was outside in the car and sent her in to make sure they were headed in the right direction, the clerk told her which way she needed to be headed in so she started out walking.

As the sun came up it got hotter and hotter so Kendra decided to try to find someone who looks safe enough to hitch-hike a ride with, she had probably walked thirty or forty minutes before a car pulled up to her asking her where she was headed and if she needed a ride. Kendra told her she missed her bus and was trying to get back to Alabama and since it was two girls and a guy she felt they were safe enough. "We can take you as far as the border. Are you hungry? It's not much but you can have some." The driver said as they pulled off.

Kendra was so happy to be leaving out of Florida and away from the Tall Dark Stranger who killed Minnie. A tear streamed down the side of her face and she smiled as she thought of the good times they had their last night together at the amusement park. "Thank you Minnie. I will never forget you for trying to help me get away. I forgive you." Kendra thought as she fell asleep.

chapter 18

Nicole lay on the sofa with the phone still clutched close to her chest when the phone rang around eight o'clock PM, there was an emergency at the hospital and she had to go in. "Can't you call someone else in"? She said in a weary voice. The voice on the other end told replied, "I know you took tonight off to be home just in case your daughter called but right now we have two registered nurses on vacation and the other two are also tending to emergencies". Nicole let out a deep sigh and told her that she needed to jump in the shower and then she'll be on the way.

After she hung up the phone, showered and grabbed her things for work; she called Ray. "Hi Ray, this is Nicole. I just got called in on an emergency, I know this is asking a lot but do you think you can come over and sit by the phone just in case I received another call tonight"? Ray told her that he is currently working the case on Pete and that it is going nowhere. "I'm finding little clues here and there but the clues just don't make sense, it's almost like someone planted them there and is staging my investigation. I'm sorry Nicole, but not tonight", Ray said sadly. Nicole asked Ray about the message from the tape recorder of which he replied, "I haven't heard anything back yet. It's going to take a while before they can filter out all the noises but I will call you as soon as I hear something back.

When she got to the hospital, it was a mad house. "What is going on"? Nicole asked. The LPN behind the desk informed her that there was shooting, someone robbed the corner mart about two hours ago and decided to shoot people to draw attention away from him and that the cops haven't caught him yet. Good thing is we haven't lost one yet; just hoping someone can give a description of the guy. "This is going to be a long night", she said as she washed her hands and checked the charts.

There were many people in the waiting area watching TV when a new news alert interrupted the movie.

A BODY WAS FOUND ON THE SIDEWALKS NOT TOO FAR FROM THE AMMUSEMENT PARK NEAR THE BOARDWALK IN FLORIDA. INVESTIGATORS HAVE RELEASED THE NAME OF THE VICTIM AND IS SAID TO BE SARAH TOOLES, A TEEN THAT WAS MISSING FOR 6 YEARS. SARAH WAS FOUND FACED DOWN WITH 3 GUNSHOT WOUNDS IN THE BACK AND 2 IN THE CHEST AND WAS PRONOUNCED DEAD ON THE SCENE. WE WILL KEEP YOU POSTED WITH UPDATES OF THIS DEVISTATING EVENT.

Nicole stood there a minute is disbelief, "Sarah Tooles, Sarah Tooles, now where have I heard that name? Oh NO!!!!!!!" she yelled and ran to the nurse's station to call Ray. He answers the phone immediately, "Yes, I just heard. I received a call from an informant that I have working with me telling me that the teen they found is the same teen whose hair sample was found in Josh's car. As far as I know; there was no one else with her so there is a good chance that Kendra is still alive if they were together. I need to make some more calls; I'll call you back soon". Nicole could not think about anything as she mentally drifted off seeing her daughters face as she stared off. Not blinking, silently questioning. "Is she alright? Is she alive"?

chapter 19

Kendra slowly opened her eyes and noticed that the car wasn't moving but was parked in the woods. "Why are we here"? She asked the driver of the car. He explained to her that they had been driving for a while and pulled off the road to get some rest. "Go back to sleep, we'll be pulling out as soon as the sun come up". Kendra looked at him, then at the two girls that were so peacefully resting. She looked at the stars and thought of her mom, tears came to her eyes as she remembered the motherly hugs she used to receive that she thought was aggravating as a teenager. "I miss those hugs", she thought as she smiled and dozed back off.

The sun rose bright, beautiful and warm on their face. The driver popped the trunk and pulled out some sandwiches and drinks from the cooler, "This ain't much but it will hold us over until we find somewhere to stop and pick up a few things". The four of them hopped out of the car, released their bladders and stretched for a little while before hopping back in the car and hitting the road. The closer she got to home; the more she smiled and thought of apologizing to her mom every day for running away. "How can anyone ever think that running away is all glamorous? I must have been out of my mind! But I'm one of the lucky ones because I'm going back home and I don't care if I'm on punishment for the rest of my life!" she giggled "Yes I do".

The ride back to Alabama seem very long, they whizzed by lots of cars, trucks and buses and sang along with almost every song that played on the radio. Kendra smiled as they drove past highway signs, "We are getting closer," she thought nervously as her mom's face popped in her mind. "The gas is getting low, we're gonna be stopping soon to gas up and grab something to eat", the driver shouted towards the back of the car because the windows were down.

They drove another thirty minutes or so before stopping to get gas at a Quick Mart. The driver got out, "Here is the card, tell them we want to fill it up and go ahead and grab some hot dogs, drinks and chips or something". The girls headed in the store, the clerk immediately ask if she could help them with something. They told her which car they were putting gas in, handed her the card and proceeded to grab the items that they needed. By the time they got to the counter; the driver had already finished pumping gas and was waiting for them outside. They put the bags in the car, hopped in and drove down the road a little to this deserted baseball park. The sun was out and it was getter hotter so he drove to the far end of the baseball park where there was lots of trees and shade.

"Okay ladies, we are going to sit here, eat our food and relax for a few minutes before hitting the road. Well, Kendra. Were you hitch-hiking a ride out of Florida and running away from something"? She felt like she could trust them; they were nice enough to offer a ride to border line. It's not quite home but; close enough. "I ran away from home", she stated as she dropped her head. "I was following up a friend, or that's what I thought she was, because I thought my mom was too demanding. She said it would be an easy life. She felt bad about everything and was trying to help me get home but was shot and died. I was alone and afraid and then I met you three". She said with a smile. The car was silent, they all looked at each other before the driver said; "So, you're a runaway huh"? Didn't anyone ever tell you that there are crazy people out here in the world that will hurt you? How do you know I'm not a psycho"? Kendra stopped eating and looked at him then at the other two before she started laughing. She stopped laughing when she noticed that no one else was laughing. "Do you have any money"? One of the female passengers asked "I know you don't think you are riding for free". Kendra shook her head no. "Well someone has to pay for your portion of the gas", the male driver sneered. Kendra told them if they can take her all the way home that her mom will be more than happy to give them money for gas and probably a little more for bringing her home. "Not good enough"! He hissed "Payment is due in full now"!

They held Kendra down as he hopped in the back seat. "We cannot take you all the way home because we are wanted. I know you will not turn us in because we will find and hurt you and your mom"! The two girls who were sitting in the back seat with her pinned her down by her wrists; Kendra fought with what little strength she had and tried to wriggle free but he punched her in the face, grabbed her by the neck and told her that if she fought back he would stab her repeatedly until she died. He told her he would make her death slow and painful. Tears started flowing down Kendra's cheeks, she thought she was safe and these were nice people but she was wrong. The male driver told the two girls to get out the car but don't go too far. The two girls looked at each other with sad stares; they knew he was hurting her because they too experience this torture. All she could think of was being home again with her mother; Kendra blacked out.

When he noticed no movement in her he called for the other two girls, they came running over. "Is she dead"? One of them asked; eyes red with tears. "We have to dump her", the male driver whispered. They drove to the far end of the park by the edge of the woods, dumped her body and threw her belongings out the car as they sped off.

REALITY OF FEAR

Kendra moaned as she slowly opened her eyes, it was getting dark. She squatted behind a tree to look around; her belongings were lying on the ground not too far from her. Kendra snuck out from behind the tree, gathered her things and eased back into the woods hoping no one saw her; she shivered. She sat on the ground, hiding from the world, ashamed of what had happened to her; "What would my mother think of me now"?

She remembered the stored they stopped at for gas and began to slowly walk in that direction, her face and body ached all over; she was hungry and cold. The walk back to the store seemed like forever, she couldn't go inside "What if they call the cops? What if they find out I'm a run away and take me to jail?" It was dark outside so she snuck around to the back of the store to see what she could find to eat in the dumpsters, she was all too familiar with doing this to survive. She found a half bottle of water with the top screwed back on, half a bag of chips and cold wrinkled hot dogs. Devouring the food from the dumpster, she felt sick and full at the same time but she was still cold so she squat down as low to the ground as she could, leaned against the building and wrapped her arms around her to keep warm.

chapter 20

Cold, dirty and alone; Kendra jumped when she heard arguing. She stayed hidden in the dark because she thought they came back to finish her off. The arguing got louder and louder so she peeped her head out just enough to see a couple getting out of their SUV and walking into the store. She ran to the truck and was going to take the woman's purse she left on the seat when she noticed the tags "ALABAMA"!!!!! She whispered. Not sure what part of Alabama they were headed but anything was worth a try she thought, and she'd be warm for a little while. She snuck in, crawled toward the back of the SUV and laid low on the floor.

The couple returned back to the truck and drove off still arguing when the woman said, "Do you smell something"? He said NO so she cracked a window and they started back arguing again. Kendra found a coat on the floor of the truck so she wrapped up in it and dozed off for what seemed like forever. When she woke up, she didn't hear any more arguing but the truck was running. She started to peep to see why they stopped but she heard moaning and lots of heavy breathing. "Oh my gosh! Did they really just stop on the side of the road to make out in the truck"? She mindfully thought. He told her he loved her and she told him she loved him too. They sat and talked for a little while after they got dressed and that's when she heard him mention where they were headed. "This is too good to be true! That's about a forty five minute drive from my house! I can easily catch a ride there and I'll be home. Oh mom, I can't wait to see you"! She thought and cried but tried not to sob out loud for fear that they would find her. Doors opened and closed and they were on their way again.

Kendra dozed back off and tried to get as much rest as she could, she knew once the truck stopped she need to get out undetected and her walk home would be long.

'HONNNNNNNK!' the man behind the wheel was blowing the horn as they pulled up to a very nice two story house. This was not a neighborhood like she lived in; the houses here were spread out almost a block apart. A loud voice came out yelling and screaming of happiness when the couple arrived. "What took y'all so long"? An elder voice asked. They all walked in the house laughing, voices loud as ever. When she could hear low, faint voices; she exited the truck taking the jacket with her to stay warm. Kendra walked up the road a while until she saw a sign that told her exactly where she was, she immediately knew which direction to walk.

It was colder in Alabama than it was in Florida, Kendra's excitement grew more and more knowing how close to home she was. She had walked a little more than thirty minutes when she came up on a small gas station that was closed; she looked for and found a payphone. She called home collect, this was the only number she could remember by hard; again no answer; again she did not leave a message. "I need to rest a little" she thought and went to the side of the store in the dark. She knew she did not need to stick around long; she found a hose to get a good drink of water and was on her way again.

Kendra staggered up the long dark road until she could go no more. Her feet were hurting and she had developed blisters on them because of the kind of shoes she had on and because she stayed walking mainly on the road but close enough to the trees so she could duck off the road if a car drove by. After the last ordeal and hitch hiking; she dared not catch a ride with anyone. "No one is to be trusted"! She said as she pressed on.

She collapsed on the side on the road; no one would stop to help her. The road was dark and long, many cars passed by where she lay on the side of the road, they thought she was either drunk or dead and wanted nothing to do with those problems so they left her there.

Kendra body was so close to the road, it's a miracle that no one ran over her. A man driving a brown pick-up truck passed her body, hit brakes and backed up. He jumped out of the truck and ran over to her, "She is still breathing"! He said in shock. The middle aged man slowly picked her up, carried her to the truck and gently slid her in the passenger side, "Hold on little missy, I will get you to a hospital as soon as possible"!

Twenty five minutes later, the brown pick-up pulled around the back-side of the hospital and carried Kendra into the emergency room entrance. "Can someone help me"! He yelled "I found her on the side of the road about thirty minutes ago. She looks like she'd been beaten pretty badly"! Three of the ER staff came running towards him, sat her in a wheel chair and wheeled her to the first room available. They checked her vital signs and to see if she was still breathing; she was so they began setting everything out for the doctor and the head nurse.

The doctor was already in the room when the nurse arrived. She stopped at the door and tears swelled in her eyes, "Oh my GOD! That's my daughter! What happened"?! The ER staff told her that a man just brought her in and said they found her on the side of the road about thirty minutes out. She looked her daughter over then turned to the doctor and asked, "Is she"? The doctor looked at Nicole and told her that she is alive and doing good considering, "She's been through a lot. We cleaned up her wounds and gave her something in her I V to help her rest. I'm sure the police would want to talk to her in the morning".

chapter 21

Nicole stepped out of the room and called Ray. "Hello"? He answered in a very groggy voice considering it is four o'clock in the morning. "Ray, it's me Nicole! My daughter was carried in to ER by a guy who found her lying on the side of the road about thirty minutes from here. No, he brought her in a left. The doctor said she is doing good considering and that the cops might want to talk to her when she's able. I want that cop to be you"! Ray was barely awaken and was trying to process all the information he just received before saying. "I'll be there as soon as I can, just make sure you stay close to her". "I will", She sniffed.

Around seven o'clock AM; Ray arrived at the hospital asked the lady at the lobby desk if she could page Nicole. He stood in the lobby for twenty minutes before she came downstairs to him. "The doctor is in the room checking her vital signs and changing bandages, they will be cleaning her up shortly. We can go up now and just wait in the lobby up there". Ray followed her to the elevator where they got off on the 6th floor. They sat in the lobby fifteen minutes when the doctor walked out, "You can go back in now. Her vitals are good and her wounds will heal but I need to tell you something first before she comes through". The doctor turns his attention to Ray before saying anything else but Nicole informed him that Ray is a detective who's been working on the case since Kendra went missing and that she called him this morning. The doctor continues talking "Because of the amount and location of the bruises; I need to show you the results of her tests". Nicole felt all life fall from her body; Ray caught her before she could hit the floor and eased her into a chair. "My poor baby"! she muttered. I need to go sit with her so I'll be the first friendly face she sees when she wakes up". She headed for the room.

Ray stood in the lobby for a few minutes and started to head to the room when his cell phone rang. "Hello? Chief? I've been trying to contact you concerning Pete's case that keeps leading me cold; there's not one drop of evidence which is strange". The Chief told Ray that he was called out of town on an emergency and will call him back if he hears anything. "Okay Chief; but I'm glad you called! An unknown man brought Kendra into the emergency room about five or six hours ago. He said he found her on the side of the road about thirty minutes out. I'm not sure which direction she was coming from so as soon as she comes through and able to talk; I'll head out and look for clues". "Great work Ray, I have another call coming in so I'll get back with you shortly to check up on her". They hang up, Ray heads to the room.

Kendra is coming through when Ray walks in. Nicole lifts her head up "Kendra, baby, it's your mom. Your safe now, I love you". Kendra opens her eyes to see her mom sitting by the bed holding her hand and a strange person standing by the window, tears begin to flow down her face. She tried to talk "Mom, mom. I'm sorry". Kendra was dehydrated; Nicole could barely understand anything she was saying. "I know baby, just rest". Kendra could not rest; she wanted her mom to hear what happened to her. Ray walked a little closer to the bed "Kendra, this is detective Ray. He's a friend who's been trying to help find you". She began to talk again, this time she spoke a little slower. Kendra tried to tell them what happened but it was all out of order that they didn't know what happened first. "Try to get a little more rest so things can come back more clear. I will talk to you again soon". She drifts back off to sleep.

Ray and Nicole stepped out of the room to try to put the puzzle together. "I think I need a cup of coffee", Ray yawned. They headed to the lobby cafeteria.

chapter 22

"May I help you sir"? The lady at the nurse's station asked. "Hi, I'm looking for Detective Ray. I am Chief Wales; we've been working on the case of the missing teen. I got a call from him this morning that she was brought in". She told him that Ray and her mom went down to the cafeteria and he should be able to catch them there. She sighed when the light went on for room 613, "I'll be right back". He thanked her and began walking towards the elevator, stopped and went back the other way towards Kendra's room and makes a call before stepping in.

The Chief steps into the hospital room where Kendra peacefully slept, stepped into the restroom and puts on a dark black cloak, large shades and black leather gloves. He walks over to the bed, she was sound asleep. "Too easy", he said picking up a pillow, smiling. Just as he placed the pillow over her face, Ray burst into the room. They tussled around the room, knocking over the small beside table, a chair and breaking the mirror on the wall by the sink .... POW! POW! POW! ......Three shots were fired; the man in the dark clothes was dead.

Ray was sitting against the wall close to the window when in rushed the doctor, a few hospital workers and Nicole who rushed to her daughter's side in tears. The doctor entered, kneeled by Ray and asked if he'd been shot. "No" Ray said breathing heavily. "Ray! That is the Tall Dark Stranger that I saw the night Josh was murdered"! Ray told her that he appear to be the same person he saw leaving Pete's garage the night it caught fire too. He pulled out his phone to call the Chief and heard a cell phone ringing. Ray slid over to the body, turned the guy over and removed the large hat and shades. "CHIEF"! "All this time I'd been calling and informing him of everything going on and it was him"! He makes a call to have the body removed and processed and told them to check his phone records for the last six months.

The doctor immediately ordered Kendra to be moved to another room as soon as possible before she wakes up, "She's been through enough, there is no need for her to know of or see this".

Kendra finally wakes up around seven-twenty PM, her mom is the first person she saw. Tears streamed down both their cheeks and Kendra told her mom that she was sorry; they both cried and expressed how much they loved and missed each other. Ray leaves mother and daughter alone and heads for the office.

A package was sitting on Ray's desk when he arrived; he eagerly opened it hoping it was the information he was waiting on .... A list of all calls made to and from the Chiefs phone. He saw the same number over and over again but whoever the number belong to, it was no longer in service. Everything about the case has gone cold; Kendra only knew the names that were presented to her when she met them. None of the information she gave Ray or her mother could be traced back to anyone and the two people that could shed some light on everything are dead.

the follow-up

Sir sat at home watching television, the news of the Chief was broadcasting over every channel. He makes a few calls, disconnects his phone and picks up a new one; packs a small bag and disappear without a trace.

Jackie did as Sir instructed, she burned the house to the ground after the Tall Dark Stranger was instructed to get rid of Minnie and Kendra. Jackie changed her name and moved on the other side of Miami, this was a better location for her. She still stays in contact with Sir.

Ray was offered the job as Chief that he took and later hired Frank on as his second in command ..... Yes, Ray brought him out of retirement.

Nicole and Kendra returned home. Per Ray's instructions; they made up a story to tell the news about Kendra's ordeal. Kendra still has nightmares to this day and is constantly receiving counseling. She and Stefanie are still the best of friends and talk every day.

COMING SOON

"KARMA"

As she walked by them; they whispered behind her back. Little did they know; she heard every word. Raged and scorned, KARMA will have her revenge!

Cover photo created by Micah J Oliver

Micah J. Oliver is from Greenville, SC and the President of G.U.R Network Media Group. Drawing has a gift that he acknowledges came from GOD, and is thankful for being able to share with the world. Oliver is also a Youth Minister at Eternal Life Christian Center located in Augusta, GA. Micah Oliver also graduated from the University of South Carolina with a Bachelor of Arts in Political Science, Minor in Speech Communications. Oliver hopes that his drawings will impact everyone in a positive way.

Micaholiver007@gmail.com